donkey trouble

Atheneum Books for Young Readers
An imprint of Simon & Schuster Children's Publishing Division
1230 Avenue of the Americas
New York, NY 10020

The text of this book is set in Cantoria Semi Bold
The illustrations were done in paper collage with pastel
Manufactured in U.S.A.
10 9 8 7 6 5 4 3 2 1

Library of Congress Cataloging-in-Publication Data

Young, Ed
   Donkey Trouble / by Ed Young.
         p.   cm.
   Summary: In this retelling of the traditional fable, a kind but simple man and his
grandson, on their way to market with their donkey, find it impossible to please
everyone they meet.
   ISBN 0-689-31854-5
   [1. Fables.] I. Title.
PZ8.2.Y68Do   1995
398.22—dc20
[E]   95-2135

donkey trouble

ED YOUNG

Atheneum Books for Young Readers

There was once a kind and simple man who lived in the desert with his kind and simple grandson. Despite hard work the old man had never prospered in life. As he grew older his possessions were fewer and fewer until finally, all he and his grandson had left was their donkey. They knew that the donkey, too, must be sold. So the three headed for the market in a town across the desert.

They had traveled only a short way when they saw two boys.
"Look at those fools," the boys jeered. "They could be riding
that donkey instead of trudging through the sand themselves."

The old man pondered this. The market was far away. "They are probably right, you know," he said, and insisted that the boy ride the animal while he walked.

The sun had risen higher in the sky when they came upon a group of travelers who were on their way to the market, too.

"What disrespect!" shouted one. "That young boy with strong legs rests on the beast while the old man struggles to pull it."

The boy looked down in shame.
"They are right, you know," he said to his grandfather.
Although his grandfather argued, the boy insisted that the
old man mount the donkey in his place.

The desert sand grew hot as they met two women returning from a well.

"What a brute," one grumbled as they approached, "causing a poor child to suffer so in this heat. . . ."

The old man and his grandson were perplexed.
"What are we to do?" they moaned. They thought and
thought and wearily arrived at a solution that seemed fair . . .

. . . until, at the edge of town a wise man came along.
"Do you know what a heavy load you are to that poor animal?"
he chided. "Carry him a ways and you'll see."

Ashamed of their unkindness, the two thought this suggestion very wise, indeed.

Word spread about the kind and simple man approaching with his kind and simple grandson.

Soon the whole town came to the river to see such a sight.

Startled by the laughter
of the crowd . . .

the donkey kicked
himself free. . .

. . .tumbled to the river, and ran off,
leaving the old man and his grandson
with nothing, nothing at all,
except for the wisdom that . . .

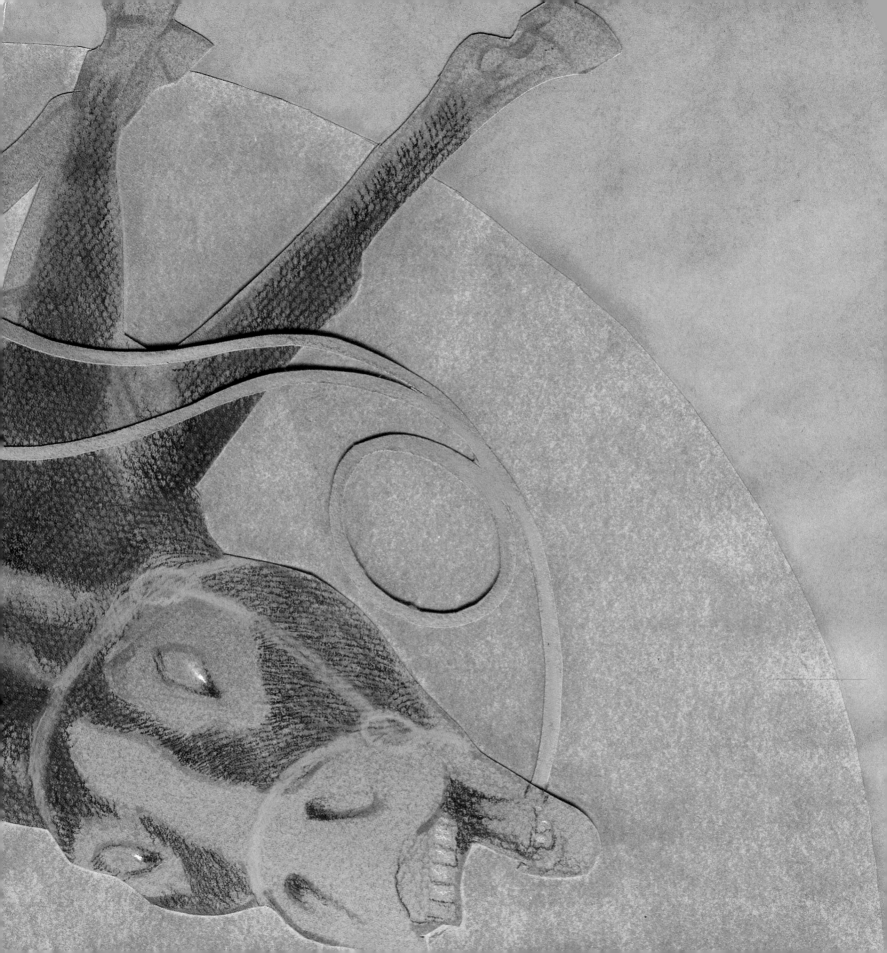

. . . to prosper,
they must follow
their own hearts.